This book belongs to:

Logan X. hellums

THE LITTLE ENGINE THAT COULD®

Retold by

WATTY PIPER

Illustrated by George & Doris Hauman

NEW YORK
PLATT & MUNK
Publishers

GROSSET & DUNLAP
An Imprint of Penguin Random House LLC, New York

Copyright © 1976, 1961, 1954, 1945, 1930 by Penguin Random House LLC. All rights reserved.
"8 Ways to Make the Most of Storytime" copyright © 2020 Meredith Corporation.
All rights reserved. Reprinted with permission.

Originally published by Platt & Munk, Publishers. This edition published by Platt & Munk,
a division of Grosset & Dunlap, an imprint of Penguin Random House LLC, in 2020.

Read Together, Be Together and the colophon, The Little Engine That Could®, I Think I Can®,
and all related titles, logos, and characters are trademarks of Penguin Random House LLC.
GROSSET & DUNLAP is a registered trademark of Penguin Random House LLC.

Visit us online at penguinrandomhouse.com.

The Library of Congress has cataloged the hardcover edition under the following Control Number: 89081287.
ISBN 978-0-448-40041-9 (hardcover) — ISBN 978-0-593-22423-6 (Read Together, Be Together)

Printed in the USA.
10 9 8 7 6 5 4 3 2 1

2020 Read Together, Be Together Edition

Chug, chug, chug. Puff, puff, puff. Ding-dong, ding-dong. The little train rumbled over the tracks.

She was a happy little train for she had such a jolly load to carry. Her cars were filled full of good things for boys and girls.

There were toy animals—giraffes with long necks, Teddy bears with almost no necks at all, and even a baby elephant.

Then there were dolls—dolls with blue eyes and yellow curls, dolls with brown eyes and brown bobbed heads, and the funniest little toy clown you ever saw.

And there were cars full of toy engines, airplanes, tops, jack-knives, picture puzzles, books, and every kind of thing boys or girls could want.

But that was not all. Some of the cars were filled with all sorts of good things for boys and girls to eat—big golden oranges, red-cheeked apples, bottles of creamy milk for their breakfasts,

fresh spinach for their dinners, peppermint drops, and lollypops for after-meal treats.

The little train was carrying all these wonderful things to the good little boys and girls on the other side of the mountain.

She puffed along merrily. Then all of a sudden she stopped with a jerk. She simply could not go another inch. She tried and she tried, but her wheels would not turn.

What were all those good little boys and girls on the other side of the mountain going to do without the wonderful toys to play with and the good food to eat?

"Here comes a shiny new engine," said the funny little clown who jumped out of the train.

"Let us ask him to help us."

So all the dolls and toys cried out together, "Please, Shiny New Engine, won't you please pull our train over the mountain? Our

engine has broken down, and the boys and girls on the other side won't have any toys to play with or good food to eat unless you help us."

But the Shiny New Engine snorted: "I pull you? I am a Passenger Engine. I have just carried a fine big train over the mountain, with more cars than you ever dreamed of. My train had sleeping cars, with comfortable berths; a dining car where waiters

bring whatever hungry people want to eat; and parlor cars in which people sit in soft armchairs and look out of big plate-glass windows. I pull the likes of you? Indeed not!"

And off he steamed to the roundhouse, where engines live when they are not busy. How sad the little train and all the dolls and toys felt!

Then the little clown called out, "The Passenger Engine is not the only one in the world. Here is another engine coming, a great big strong one. Let us ask him to help us."

The little toy clown waved his flag and the big strong engine came to a stop.

"Please, oh, please, Big Engine," cried all the dolls and toys together. "Won't you please pull our train over the mountain?

Our engine has broken down, and the good little boys and girls on the other side won't have any toys to play with or good food to eat unless you help us."

But the Big Strong Engine bellowed: "I am a Freight Engine. I have just pulled a big train loaded with big machines over the mountain. These machines print books and newspapers for grown-ups

to read. I am a very important engine indeed. I won't pull the likes of you!" And the Freight Engine puffed off indignantly to the roundhouse.

The little train and all the dolls and toys were very sad.

"Cheer up," cried the little toy clown. "The Freight Engine is not the only one in the world. Here comes another. He looks very

old and tired, but our train is so little, perhaps he can help us."

So the little toy clown waved his flag and the dingy, rusty old engine stopped.

"Please, Kind Engine," cried all the dolls and toys together. "Won't you please pull our train over the mountain? Our engine has broken down, and the boys and girls on the other side won't have any toys to play with or good food to eat unless you help us."

But the Rusty Old Engine sighed, "I am so tired. I must rest

my weary wheels. I cannot pull even so little a train as yours over the mountain. I can not. I can not. I can not."

And off he rumbled to the roundhouse chugging, "I can not. I can not. I can not."

Then indeed the little train was very, very sad, and the dolls and toys were ready to cry.

But the little clown called out, "Here is another engine coming, a little blue engine, a very little one, maybe she will help us."

The very little engine came chug, chugging merrily along. When she saw the toy clown's flag, she stopped quickly.

"What is the matter, my friends?" she asked kindly.

"Oh, Little Blue Engine," cried the dolls and toys. "Will you pull us over the mountain? Our engine has broken down and the good boys and girls on the other side won't have any toys to play

with or good food to eat, unless you help us. Please, please help us,
Little Blue Engine."

"I'm not very big," said the Little Blue Engine. "They use me only for switching trains in the yard. I have never been over the mountain."

"But we must get over the mountain before the children

awake," said all the dolls and the toys.

The very little engine looked up and saw the tears in the dolls' eyes. And she thought of the good little boys and girls on the other side of the mountain who would not have any toys or good food unless she helped.

Then she said, "I think I can. I think I can. I think I can." And she hitched herself to the little train.

She tugged and pulled and pulled and tugged and slowly, slowly, slowly they started off.

The toy clown jumped aboard and all the dolls and the toy animals began to smile and cheer.

Puff, puff, chug, chug, went the Little Blue Engine. "I think I can—I think I can—I think I can—I think I can—I think I can—I think I can—I think I can—I think I can—I think I can."

Up, up, up. Faster and faster and faster the little engine climbed, until at last they reached the top of the mountain.

Down in the valley lay the city.

"Hurray, hurray," cried the funny little clown and all the dolls and toys. "The good little boys and girls in the city will be happy because you helped us, kind Little Blue Engine."

And the Little Blue Engine smiled and seemed to say as she puffed steadily down the mountain...

"I thought I could. I thought I could. I thought I could. I thought I could.

I thought I could.

I thought I could."

8 Ways to Make the Most of Storytime

FROM THE EDITORS OF
Parents.

1
BE AS DRAMATIC AS POSSIBLE.

It'll help the story stick in your child's memory. You could give the mouse a British accent, make the lion roar, or speak very slowly when you're reading the snail's dialogue. Have fun making sound effects for words like boom, moo, or achoo. Encourage your child to act out movements, slithering like a snake or leaping like a frog.

2
INVITE SPECIAL GUESTS.

Ask your kids if their favorite stuffed animal, action figure, or doll would like to listen too. Or curl up with the family pet. Including the whole gang will help hold their interest and make storytime seem more special. But if your child does start to lose interest before you've reached the last page, that's okay because half a book here or a quarter of a book there still counts as reading!

3
KEEP LOVINGLY WORN BOOKS IN THE ROTATION.

There's a reason your kids ask for the same title again and again: A familiar story can be as comforting as a favorite blankie. The characters become their friends, and the books serve an important emotional purpose.

4
PLAY A GUESSING GAME.

When reading a new book, pause a few times to challenge your kids to predict what's going to happen next. Encourage them to refer to the title and illustrations for clues.

5
REFLECT ON THE STORY.

Talk about a book for a few minutes before you move on to another. Start a conversation with statements like "I'm wondering…," "I wish I could ask the author…," and "I'm getting the idea…" This helps develop your children's intuition and their ability to communicate a story back to you.

READ TOGETHER, BE TOGETHER

is a nationwide movement developed by Penguin Random House in partnership with *Parents* magazine that celebrates the importance, and power, of the shared reading experience between an adult and a child. Reading aloud regularly to babies and young children is one of the most effective ways to foster early literacy and is a key factor responsible for building language and social skills. READ TOGETHER, BE TOGETHER offers parents the tips and tools to make family reading a regular and cherished activity.

6
CONNECT STORIES WITH WHAT'S HAPPENING IN REAL LIFE.

Suppose you read your child a story about a baby bird, and a day or two later, you spot a tiny sparrow in the park. Ask your child, "Doesn't that bird look like the one in the book we read yesterday? I wonder if it's looking for its mommy too?" Doing so will help promote information recall and build vocabulary.

7
CREATE AN IMPROVISED READING NOOK.

Storytime on the sofa or a cozy chair is sweet, but wouldn't your kids lose their mind if you set up a fort every now and then? It doesn't have to be fancy: Just drape a blanket over two chairs, grab a couple of pillows, and squeeze in.

8
ALWAYS BE THE STORYTELLER AT BEDTIME.

You'll feel so proud when your little ones start recognizing and sounding out words on their own. But resist asking them to read to you at bedtime because it would replace this warm, wonderful bonding ritual with something that can feel like work for kids. Plus, they'll be able to listen to a more complicated book than they can read on their own.